# Sleeping Beauty

## With Selected Sentences
## in American Sign Language

Adaptation and Art Direction by Robert Newby

Story Illustrations by Pat Steiner
Sign Illustrations by Sandra Cozzolino

FOREST HOUSE ™
School & Library Edition

Kendall Green Publications
Gallaudet University Press
Washington, D.C.

**Kendall Green Publications**
An imprint of Gallaudet University Press
Washington, DC 20002-3695

© 1992 by Gallaudet University. All rights reserved
Published 1992
Printed in Singapore

*Library of Congress Cataloging-in-Publication Data*

Newby, Robert, 1932-
    Sleeping Beauty: with selected sentences in American Sign Language /
adaption and art direction by Robert Newby; illustrations by Pat Steiner;
line drawings by Sandra Cozzolino.
    p. cm.
    Summary: Retells the familiar fairy tale in English and American Sign
Language. Includes information about ASL and how it is used.
    ISBN 0-930323-97-1
    [1. Fairy tales.    2. Folklore.    3. Sign language.] I. Steiner, Pat,
ill.    II. Cozzolono, Sandra, ill.    III. Sleeping Beauty. English.
IV. Title.
PZ8.N42S1 1992
398.21—dc20                                                      91-29729
                                                                      CIP
                                                                       AC

# Sleeping Beauty

With Selected Sentences
in American Sign Language

# Introduction

AMERICAN Sign Language, called ASL, is a fun and exciting language! Because deaf people cannot hear spoken language, some learn ASL to communicate with other deaf people and with hearing people who know sign. ASL is a language, like English, Spanish, or French. Signs are used like words are used in spoken languages.

Some ASL signs can't be translated into English, nor can some English words be translated into signs. English words that can't be signed are spelled using the fingers of one hand. This is called *fingerspelling*; the hand forms the letters of the *manual alphabet.* By looking at the manual alphabet on the opposite page, you can tell that some of the letters in the manual alphabet look like written letters. Numbers are signed using the *manual numbers*, also shown on the opposite page.

Some signs are made using one hand and some are made using two hands. Usually people use the hand that they write and eat with to sign the one-handed signs and to fingerspell. When making two-handed signs use the hand you write with to make the main movement. The signs in this book are drawn for right-handed people. If you are left-handed, reverse the signs.

Using your face and body to help express what you are signing is an important part of ASL. Sometimes, the face expresses as much information as the signs. If deaf people are signing *"love"*, a big smile lights up their faces. Or, if they are signing *"angry"*, a frown crosses their faces. Quite often, when people ask a question in English, their faces change. Their eyebrows move up, their eyes open

BEAUTY  ISOBEL

ONE HUNDRED

wide, and their foreheads crinkle. Deaf people do the same thing, but to a greater degree because face and body movements are part of ASL.

Signs are made using handshapes. Some handshapes use the letters from the manual alphabet or manual numbers, but there are special handshapes too. Special handshapes can be used for *name signs*, which deaf people use to identify each other. Sometimes, name signs use the handshape from the first letter of the person's name and sometimes the name sign uses a pleasant feature of the person's appearance. Look at two name signs from our story, *Sleeping Beauty*.

The order of words in ASL is different than the order in English. Words that describe are called adjectives; for example, *beautiful, old, kind, bright,* and *one hundred* are some of the adjectives used in our story. In spoken and written English, the adjectives usually appear before the noun, for example, the beautiful girl. In ASL, however, the most important word is identified first and then the adjectives can appear before or sometimes after the noun. There are many adjectives in *Sleeping Beauty* that describe people, places, or things....how many can you find?

This is only a short introduction to ASL. It is a beautiful language to watch and to sign. With practice, you can learn enough to tell a story, too!

Have fun with *Sleeping Beauty* and with learning some American Sign Language! There is a videotape about *Sleeping Beauty* that has a deaf actor showing more about ASL and telling the story, too. You can order the videotape or purchase it from your bookstore.

# The Manual Alphabet

A    B    C    D    E    F    G    H    I

J    K    L    M    N    O    P    Q

R    S    T    U    V    W    X    Y    Z

# Numbers

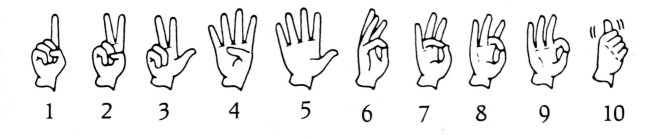

1    2    3    4    5    6    7    8    9    10

KING      QUEEN      HAVE

BEAUTIFUL      BABY      GIRL

NAME      BEAUTY.

King Alphonse and Queen Gertrude had a beautiful baby girl, and they named her Beauty.

ONCE upon a time, in a tiny kingdom called Sera, lived a King and Queen.
King Alphonse and Queen Gertrude had a beautiful baby girl, and they named her
Beauty.

The King and Queen loved Princess Beauty very much. All the people of Sera
loved her, too.

KING

QUEEN

PLAN

BIG

PARTY

CELEBRATION

BIRTHDAY

BEAUTY.

The King and Queen planned a big party to celebrate the birth of the Princess.

THE King and Queen planned a big party to celebrate the birth of the Princess.
   King Alphonse prepared the guest list and Queen Gertrude chose the food. Of course, the Queen picked out a new dress.

PEOPLE  EVERYWHERE  COME-TO  PARTY.

PEOPLE  SIT  LONG-HALL  EAT

ENJOY  ADMIRE  BEAUTY.

Most of the people in the kingdom came to the party. Everyone sat in the Great Hall to eat and to admire the new Princess.

THE cooks in the castle kitchen prepared a wonderful feast. Most of the people in the kingdom came to the party. Everyone sat in the Great Hall to eat and to admire the new Princess.

ALL-FOUR-OF-US

GIFTS-GIFTS

BABY

BEAUTY.

GIFTS

WHAT?

BLESSINGS

AND

GOOD

FUTURE

FOR

BABY

BEAUTY.

"We each brought a gift for the baby Princess. Our gifts are blessings and good wishes for Beauty."

FIVE Good Fairies lived in Sera. They had delicate wings like butterflies. Four of the Good Fairies came to the party.

A Wicked Fairy also lived in the kingdom. Everyone was afraid of her. The King and Queen did not invite the Wicked Fairy to the party.

After the feast, the first Good Fairy told the King and Queen, "We each brought a gift for the baby Princess. Our gifts are blessings and good wishes for Beauty."

BEAUTY WILL HAVE WONDERFUL

LIFE BECAUSE THOSE GOOD

FAIRIES' BLESSINGS.

Beauty would have a wonderful life because of the Good Fairies' blessings.

THE first Good Fairy blessed Beauty with kindness, and the second Good Fairy gave her health. The third Good Fairy's gift was beauty.

The last Good Fairy gave Beauty happiness. Then she blessed Beauty. The Good Fairy said, "May you grow up kind and beautiful. May you be happy and healthy."

The King and Queen were very happy. Beauty would have a wonderful life because of the Good Fairies' blessings. The Good Fairies waved good-bye and flew away.

BAD

FAIRY

FLY

IN

WINDOW.

YOU

NOT-YET

INVITE

ME

PARTY

BUT

ME

HAVE

GIFT

FOR

BABY

TOO.

The Wicked Fairy flew in the window. "You did not invite me to the party! But I have a gift for the baby, too."

SUDDENLY, a scream filled the Great Hall. All the people were frightened! The Wicked Fairy flew in the window. She screamed at the King and Queen, "You did not invite me to the party! But I have a gift for the baby, too."

BAD

FAIRY

POINT-AT

BEAUTY.

MY

GIFT

WHAT?

BAD

MAGIC.

SPINNING-WHEEL

BEAUTY

WILL

PRICK-FINGER

BLEED

DIE.

The Wicked Fairy pointed her long finger at Beauty."My gift is not a blessing. It is a curse! Beauty will prick her finger on a spinning wheel and she will die!"

THE Wicked Fairy pointed her long finger at Beauty. "My gift is not a blessing. It is a wicked wish. My gift is a curse!"

"Beauty will grow up kind and beautiful and healthy." The Wicked Fairy's voice became louder. "But, on her sixteenth birthday, Beauty will prick her finger on a spinning wheel. Her finger will bleed and she will die!"

The Wicked Fairy turned and flew out the window.

DON'T AFRAID BAD FAIRY

BAD MAGIC. ME HELP-YOU.

ME WILL CHANGE BAD

MAGIC WITH MY GIFT-BLESSING.

"Do not be afraid of the Wicked Fairy's curse. I will help you. I can change the curse with my blessing."

SHOCKED and frightened, King Alphonse and Queen Gertrude watched the Wicked Fairy fly away. Then Beauty began to cry. The Queen hurried to protect her new baby. The King comforted the Queen. They did not know what to do.

Just then, the King felt a tap on his shoulder. He turned and saw another Good Fairy, the smallest of them all.

The Good Fairy said, "My name is Isobel. I am late for the party, but I am glad that I arrived now. Do not be afraid of the Wicked Fairy's curse. I will help you. I can change the curse with my blessing."

ON · 16 · BIRTHDAY · BEAUTY

WILL · PRICK-FINGER · BUT · WILL

NOT · DIE. · BEAUTY · SLEEP

CONTINUOUS · ONE · HUNDRED · YEARS.

On her sixteenth birthday, she will prick her finger on a spinning wheel, but she will not die. She will sleep for one hundred years.

ISOBEL explained, "My gift for Beauty is long life. Beauty will grow up happy and healthy. On her sixteenth birthday, she will prick her finger on a spinning wheel, but she will not die. She will fall asleep and wake up again."

"How long will Beauty sleep?" asked King Alphonse.

"She will sleep for one hundred years," Isobel answered. "Then a handsome young Prince will find her. The Prince will kiss Beauty and she will awaken."

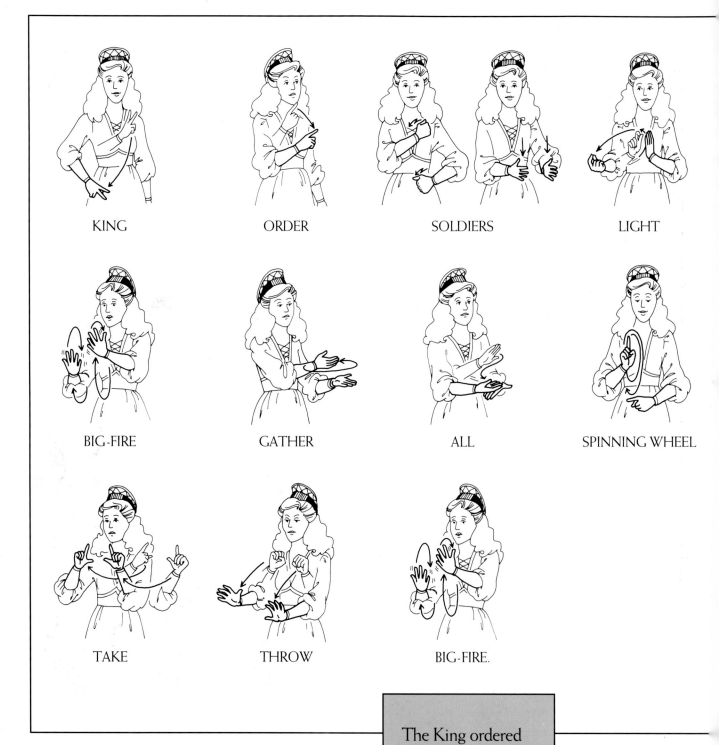

KING      ORDER      SOLDIERS      LIGHT

BIG-FIRE      GATHER      ALL      SPINNING WHEEL

TAKE      THROW      BIG-FIRE.

The King ordered his men to find all the spinning wheels in the kingdom and to make a big fire and to burn the spinning wheels.

KING Alphonse and Queen Gertrude worried for several days. Then the Queen said, "I do not want Beauty to sleep for one hundred years. Can we stop this from happening?"

The King answered, "I will think about it. We must do something."

The King thought of a plan. He ordered his men to find all the spinning wheels in the kingdom and to bring them to the castle. Then the King told his men to make a big fire and to burn the spinning wheels.

"Now Beauty will be safe," he told the Queen.

BEAUTY GROW-UP BECOME BEAUTIFUL

YOUNG WOMAN. SHE VERY

KIND.

Beauty became a beautiful young woman. She was very kind.

BEAUTY became a beautiful young woman. She was very kind. Her cheeks glowed with good health. She made many people happy.

The King and Queen watched Beauty grow and change. They were very proud of their fine daughter.

BEAUTY

PEEK

BEHIND-DOOR

SEE

OLD

STAIRS.

CURIOUS

CLIMB-STAIRS.

Beauty peeked behind the door and saw some crumbling stairs. Beauty was curious and she slowly climbed the stairs.

ON her sixteenth birthday, Beauty wandered down a hallway in the castle. She had never seen this hallway before. She found a heavy old door that was partly open.

Beauty peeked behind the door and saw some crumbling stairs. Beauty was curious and she slowly climbed the stairs. At the top was another door.

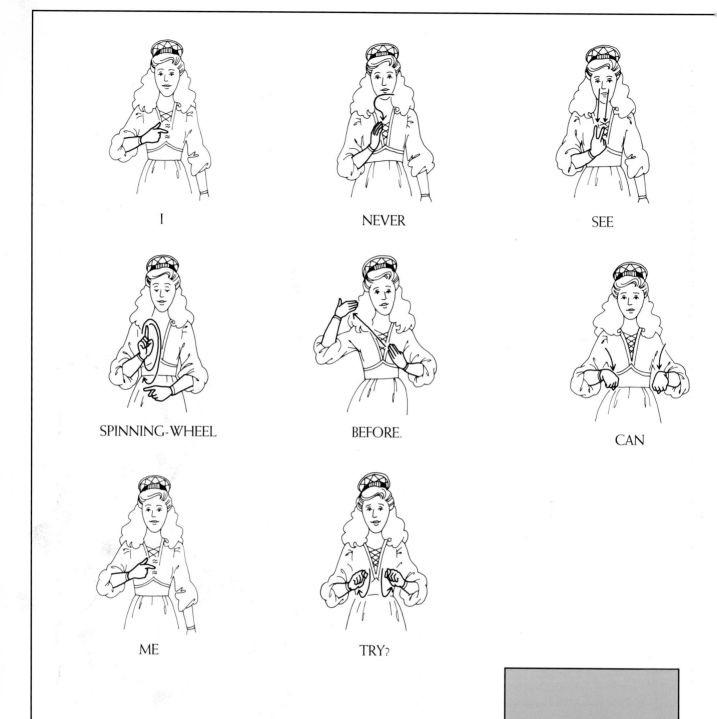

I

NEVER

SEE

SPINNING-WHEEL

BEFORE.

CAN

ME

TRY?

"I have never seen a spinning wheel before. May I try it?"

BEAUTY opened the door. She walked into a small room at the very top of the castle. An old woman sat at a spinning wheel. The old woman was spinning wool into yarn.

   The old woman turned and smiled. "Good morning, Beauty," she said. "Please come in. Come and see my spinning wheel."

   Beauty said, "I have never seen a spinning wheel before. May I try it?"

   The old woman answered cheerfully, "Yes, Beauty. Of course you may."

BEAUTY

SIT-DOWN

SPINNING WHEEL.

PRICK-FINGER.

Beauty sat down
at the spinning
wheel. The moment
she touched it, she
pricked her finger!

BEAUTY sat down at the spinning wheel. The moment she touched it, she pricked her finger! She cried out, "Help me, old woman! I pricked my finger and it is bleeding!" But the old woman did not help Beauty. She only smiled.

BEAUTY

FALL-ASLEEP.

OLD

WOMAN

CHANGE

SELF

BAD

FAIRY.

Beauty quickly fell into a deep sleep. The old woman turned into her true self, the Wicked Fairy.

BEAUTY quickly fell into a deep sleep.

The old woman turned into her true self, the Wicked Fairy. She cackled and said, "Now my curse will come true. Beauty, you will die!" The Wicked Fairy flew up and out the window.

But Beauty was not dead. She was only sleeping. The Wicked Fairy did not know about Isobel's gift.

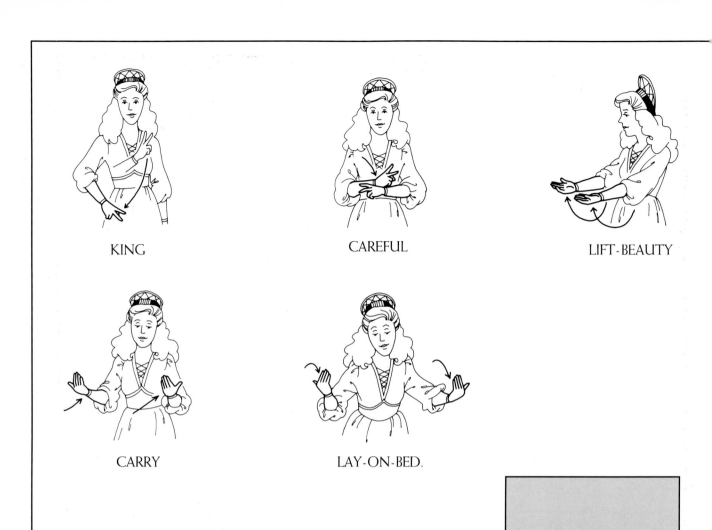

KING

CAREFUL

LIFT-BEAUTY

CARRY

LAY-ON-BED.

King Alphonse himself gently carried Beauty to her bed.

THE King's men found Beauty asleep in the room at the top of the castle. The King ordered them to bring Beauty's bed to the Great Hall. King Alphonse himself gently carried Beauty to her bed.

King Alphonse comforted Queen Gertrude, "Do not be afraid. Beauty is only sleeping. Remember that she will sleep for one hundred years. Then a young Prince will find her and she will wake up. Let us be thankful for Isobel's gift."

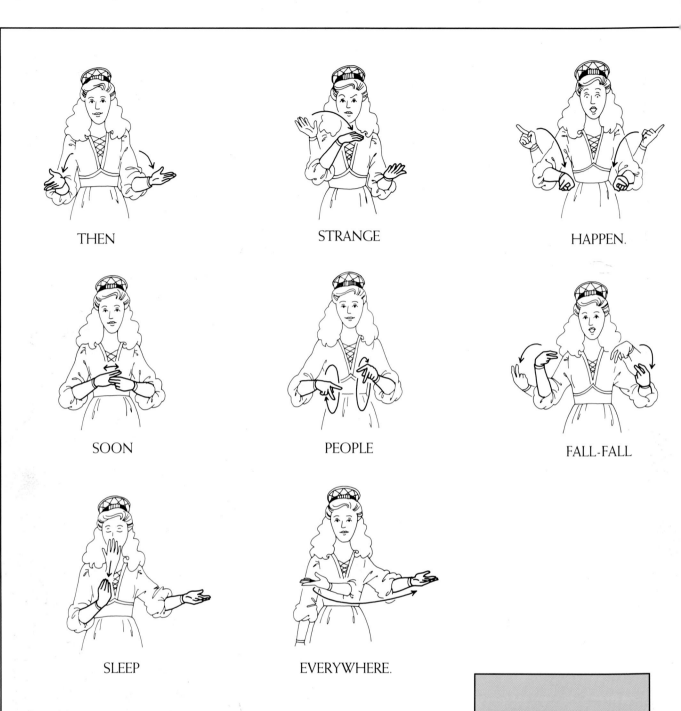

THEN STRANGE HAPPEN.

SOON PEOPLE FALL-FALL

SLEEP EVERYWHERE.

Then, a strange thing happened. Soon, everyone in the castle fell asleep, too.

$T$HEN, a strange thing happened. Soon, everyone in the castle fell asleep, too.
   Vines began to grow up the walls and across the floors.
   Everything was quiet.

CASTLE

TREES

VINES

GROW-UP-WALLS.

The trees surrounding the castle grew taller and taller, and the vines covered the castle walls.

Everyone outside the castle fell asleep, too. Even the dogs, the cats, the horses, and the chickens were sleeping.

The trees surrounding the castle grew taller and taller, and the vines covered the castle walls.

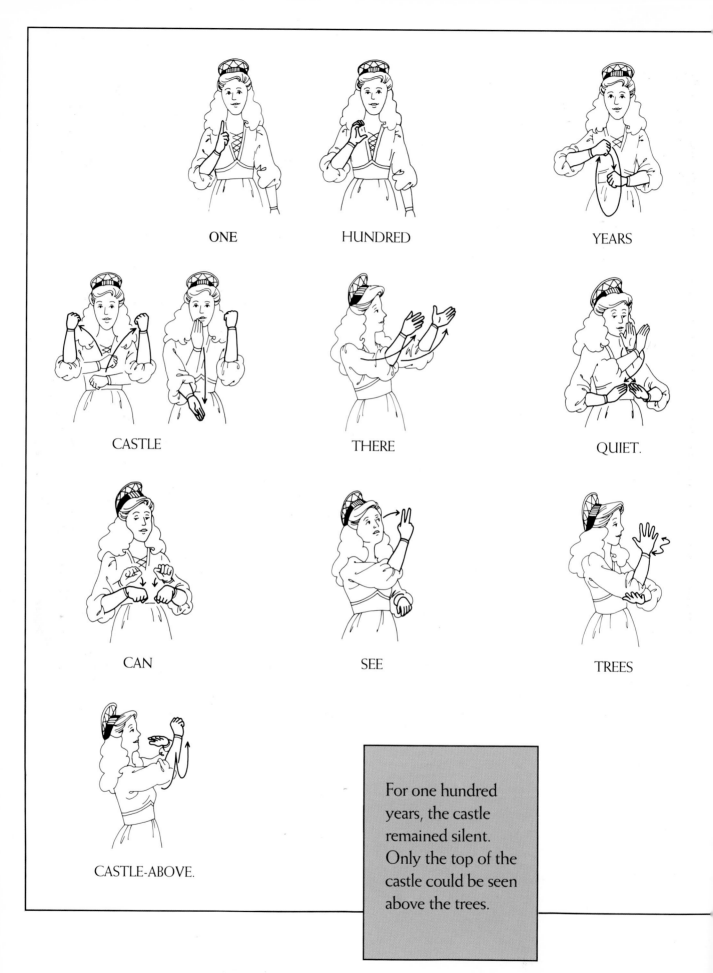

ONE HUNDRED YEARS

CASTLE THERE QUIET.

CAN SEE TREES

CASTLE-ABOVE.

For one hundred years, the castle remained silent. Only the top of the castle could be seen above the trees.

FOR one hundred years, the castle remained silent. Only the top of the castle could be seen above the trees.

No one came near the castle.

ONE-DAY

HANDSOME

PRINCE

RIDE

THROUGH

TREES-MANY.

HAPPEN

FAIRY

APPEAR.

ME

GOOD

FAIRY

ISOBEL.

Then one day, a handsome Prince was riding in the woods. Suddenly, Isobel appeared. "I am the Good Fairy Isobel."

THEN one day, a handsome Prince was riding in the woods. He saw the very top of the castle sticking out from the trees and vines. He was amazed and curious.

Suddenly, Isobel appeared. "Who are you?" asked the Prince, surprised.

"I am the Good Fairy Isobel," she answered.

The Prince told Isobel, "My name is Prince Brinwood." Then he asked, "Do you live in that castle in the trees?"

"No," Isobel replied, "a beautiful young Princess named Beauty lives there. She and everyone in the castle have been sleeping for one hundred years. They have been waiting for you to take away the curse of the Wicked Fairy."

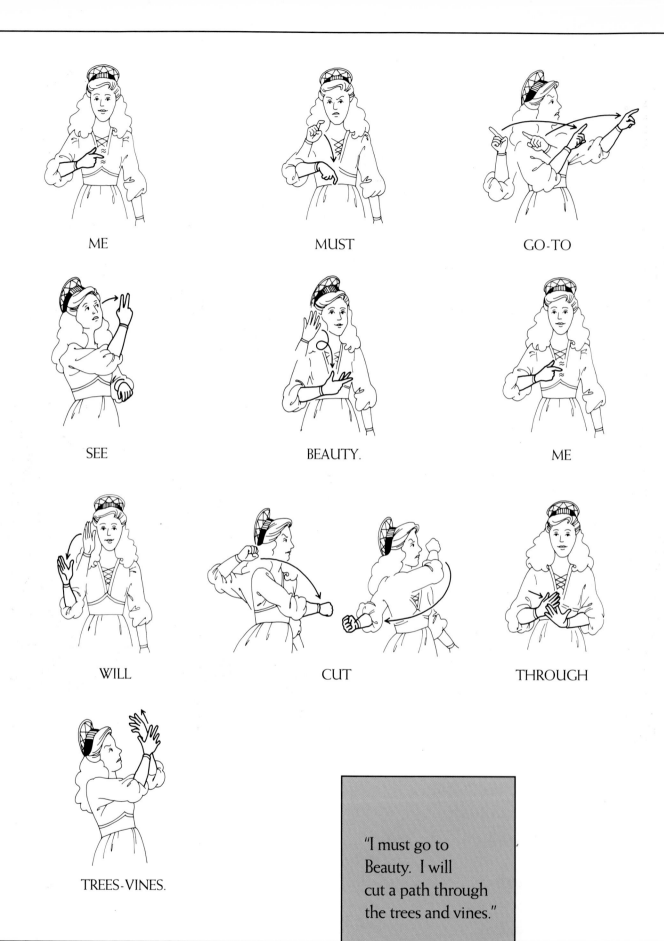

ME

MUST

GO-TO

SEE

BEAUTY.

ME

WILL

CUT

THROUGH

TREES-VINES.

"I must go to
Beauty.  I will
cut a path through
the trees and vines."

PRINCE Brinwood said in a strong voice, "I must go to Beauty. I will cut a path through the trees and vines."

Isobel said, "I will help you." And she waved her hand. Some of the trees moved to the left and some moved to the right. The vines turned away from the path.

The Prince ran toward the castle.

PRINCE        ARRIVE        CASTLE.

MEN        WOMEN        FALL-ASLEEP        EVERYWHERE.

VINES

EVERYWHERE.

Prince Brinwood came to the castle. Men and women were sprawled on the grass asleep. Vines were everywhere.

PRINCE Brinwood came to the castle. He knew that everyone was sleeping, but he was still shocked! Men and women were sprawled on the grass asleep. The dogs and cats and chickens slept peacefully.

No one and nothing moved. Vines were everywhere.

PRINCE     RAN     PAST

SOLDIERS     FALL-FALL     UP-TO-DOORS.

PUSH-PUSH     OPEN

Prince Brinwood hurried past the soldiers and pushed on the castle doors. Slowly, the doors opened.

THE soldiers guarding the castle doors were deep asleep. Prince Brinwood hurried past the soldiers and pushed on the castle doors.

The heavy doors did not move. They had not been opened for many years. The Prince used all his strength and pushed as hard as he could.

Slowly, the doors opened.

LONG-HALL     PRINCE     SEE     BEAUTY

THERE     SLEEP.

In the Great Hall
he found Beauty
in a deep sleep.

PRINCE Brinwood walked in and looked around at the castle. In the Great Hall he found Beauty in a deep sleep.

The Prince cried out, "Ah, Beauty, you are so lovely!"

PRINCE

WALK-TO

BED.

LEAN-OVER

KISS-BEAUTY-ON-
CHEEK.

The Prince walked
quietly to the bed.
He leaned over
and kissed Beauty
on the cheek.

THE Prince walked quietly to the bed. He leaned over and kissed Beauty on the cheek. Beauty's eyes fluttered and then began to open.

BEAUTY

SIT-UP

LOOK-UP

SMILE

BRIGHT.

MY

PRINCE

YOU

COME-TO-ME.

ME

DREAM

YOU

CONTINUOUS

ONE

HUNDRED

YEARS.

Beauty sat up and smiled brightly at Prince Brinwood. "My Prince, you have come to me. I have dreamed of you for one hundred years."

BEAUTY sat up and smiled brightly at Prince Brinwood. The Prince gently took her hand and gazed into her eyes.

Beauty said, "My Prince, you have come to me. I have dreamed of you for one hundred years."

Everyone in the castle woke up and stretched. They began to talk and to move around again.

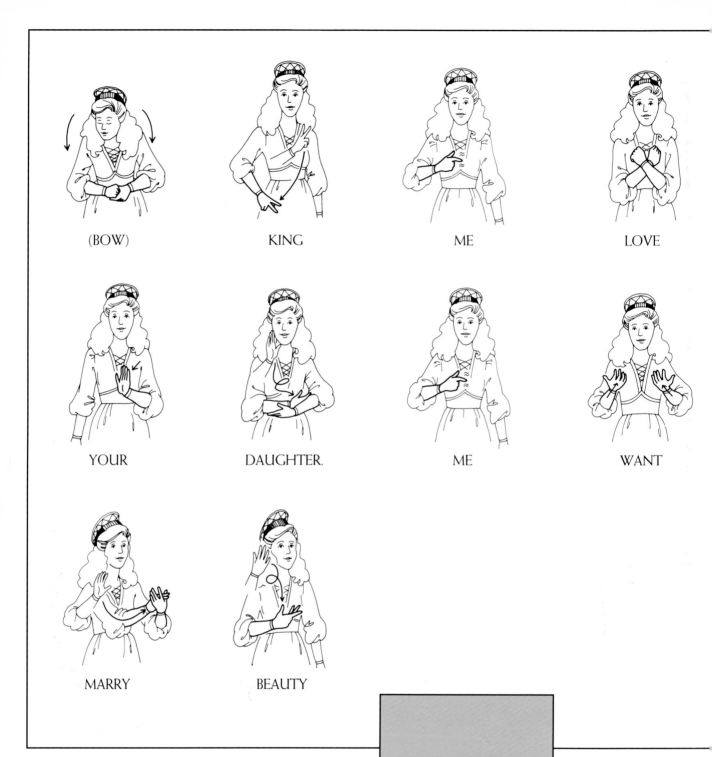

(BOW)  KING  ME  LOVE

YOUR  DAUGHTER.  ME  WANT

MARRY  BEAUTY

"King Alphonse,
I love your daughter.
I wish to marry her."

KING Alphonse and Queen Gertrude were delighted to see Beauty and the handsome young Prince.

The Prince said, "King Alphonse, I love your daughter. I wish to marry her."

The King and Queen smiled. The King answered, "Certainly, you may marry Beauty."

BEAUTY     PRINCE     MEET     MARRY.

FIVE     GOOD     FAIRIES     COME-TO

WEDDING.     ISOBEL     GIVE     BLESSING

TWO-OF-THEM.

Beauty married Prince Brinwood. The five Good Fairies came to the wedding and Isobel blessed the Prince and Princess.

BEAUTY married Prince Brinwood. The King and Queen invited all the people in the kingdom to the wedding. Of course, they did not invite the Wicked Fairy. She had died when Beauty awakened.

The five Good Fairies came to the wedding and Isobel blessed the Prince and Princess. Everyone in the tiny kingdom of Sera was filled with happiness and joy.

Beauty and Prince Brinwood lived happily together for a long, long time.

*Children can learn more about sign language and deafness from the following books and videotapes:*

**Buffy's Orange Leash** *by Stephen Golder and Lise Memling, illustrated by Marcy Ramsey.* Buffy, a Hearing Dog, helps the Johnson family by alerting them to sounds like the telephone and doorbell, even when their young son Billy is crying.
*ISBN 0-930323-42-4, 8 1/2 x 7 hardcover, 32 pages, full-color illustrations.*

**Discovering Sign Language** *by Laura Greene and Eva B. Dicker.* Children learn all about hearing loss, different sign language systems, games, and "How the Seasons Came to Be," a story in sign for elementary-age children.
*ISBN 0-930323-48-3, 5 1/4 x 8 1/4 softcover, 104 pages, line drawings.*

**I Can Sign My ABCs** *by Susan Chaplin, illustrated by Laura McCaul.* This full-color book has 26 signs, each with its manual alphabet handshape followed by the picture, the name, and the sign for a simple object beginning with that letter, an ideal book for teaching both the English and the American Manual alphabets.
*ISBN 0-930323-19-X, 7 x 7 1/2 hardcover, 56 pages, full-color illustrations.*

**King Midas With Selected Sentences in American Sign Language** *adapted by Robert Newby, illustrated by Dawn Majewski and Sandy Cozzolino.* This classic, fully illustrated, tale of King Midas, who turns everything he touches into gold, is told accompanied by line drawings of 44 selected sentences in American Sign Language, and 120 signs for different vocabulary words.
*ISBN 0-930323-75-0, 8 1/2 x 11 hardcover, 64 pages, full-color illustrations, line drawings.*

**King Midas Videotape**, the companion to the book, features renowned deaf actor Mike Lamitola first explaining in sign language ten key sentences and signs for important vocabulary words. Then, while dressed in full costume, he signs and performs the complete story, showing the full elegance and beauty of American Sign Language.
*ISBN 0-930323-71-8, VHS, 30 minutes, ISBN 0-930323-77-7, book and videotape.*

**Little Red Riding Hood Told in Signed English** *by Harry Bornstein and Karen L. Saulnier, illustrated by Bradley O. Pomeroy.* One of the most loved folktales is told through text and drawings of Signed English, the system that uses American Sign Language signs to give children a strong grasp of English grammar and vocabulary.
*ISBN 0-930323-63-7, 8 1/2 x 11 hardcover, 48 pages, full-color illustrations, line drawings.*

**My First Book of Sign** *by Pamela J. Baker, illustrated by Patricia Bellan Gillen.* This alphabet book gives the signs for the 150 words most frequently used by young children. The text includes complete explanations on how to form each sign.
*ISBN 0-930323-20-3, 9 x 12 harcover, full-color illustrations.*

**My Signing Book of Numbers** *by Patricia Bellan Gillen.* Children can learn their numbers in sign language from this book, which has the appropriate number of things or creatures for numbers 0 through 20, 30, 40, 50, 60, 70, 80, 90, 100, and 1,000.
*ISBN 0-930323-37-8, 9 x 12 hardcover, 56 pages, full-color illustrations, line drawings.*

**Now I Understand** *by Gregory S. LaMore, illustrated by Jan Ensing-Keelan.* At first, the new boy's schoolmates don't understand why he never answers their questions, and they become angry. Then, the teacher explains that he is hard of hearing, which helps the children to understand about hearing loss and "mainstreaming."
ISBN 0-930323-13-0, *5 1/2 x 8 1/2 flexicover, 52 pages, full-color illustrations.*

**Nursery Rhymes from Mother Goose Told in Signed English** *by Harry Bornstein and Karen L. Saulnier, illustrated by Patricia Peters, sign illustrations by Linda Tom.* More than a dozen favorite verses are illustrated in color, and the text also is told through line drawings of Signed English. Children discover the fun of rhyme while also strengthening their language skills.
*ISBN 0-930323-99-8, 8 1/2 x 11 hardcover, 48 pages, full color illustrations.*

**A Very Special Friend** *by Dorothy Hoffman Levi, illustrated by Ethel Gold.* Frannie, who is six, finds a very special friend. She meets Laura, who "talks" in sign language. Laura teaches Frannie signing, and they become fast friends.
*ISBN 0-930323-55-6, 8 1/2 x 7 hardcover, 32 pages, full-color illustrations.*

**A Very Special Sister** *by Dorothy Hoffman Levi, illustrated by Ethel Gold.* Laura, who is deaf, hopes that her mother's new baby is a girl. Then Laura begins to worry that her mother will love the baby more if the baby can hear.
*ISBN 0-930323-96-3, 8 1/2 x 11 hardcover, 32 pages, full-color illustrations.*

***You can order these books at your local bookstore or by calling toll-free 1-800-451-1073.***